AF154996

The Beautiful Spanish Girl

Sexy Erotic Stories for Adults Illustrated with Hentai Pictures

_____

Emily White

Copyright © 2024 by **Emily White**

All rights reserved. No part of this book may be reproduced or transmitted in any form or by any means without written permission from the author.

Printing and distribution: Heinz-Beusen-Stieg 5 22926 Ahrensburg, Germany

TABLE OF CONTENTS

INTRODUCTION

Welcome to a captivating journey where my enthralling stories seamlessly intertwine with enchanting illustrations that redefine the very essence of desire in the world of hentai erotica.

Within the secret pages of these forbidden tales, I invite you to immerse yourself in a fiery universe of unrestrained passion. Every word is a whispered moan, and each illustration is a visual embrace that transforms the realms of fantasy into tangible reality.

This collection is not for the faint of heart. It's a bold manifesto, an invitation urging you to delve into the dark depths of lust, where pleasure is painted with audacious strokes and details that promise to quicken the rhythm of your heart. The illustrations are provocative gateways, guiding you into sensual dimensions where every hidden desire finds its expression without remorse.

Are you ready to plunge into a whirlwind of seduction and temptation, where the pages themselves transform into a stage for your most secret fantasies? Allow yourself to be carried away into a realm where sin transforms into art, and art seamlessly merges harmoniously with the ecstasy of desire.

Lift the cover and prepare for an experience ignited by the flame of passion. This is not just another collection; it's your exclusive ticket to the boldest manifestations of anime eros, written masterfully by me, **Emily White**.

THE BEAUTIFUL SPANISH GIRL

Flavie and I met one evening at our friend Fay's house. We met her at a dinner at the restaurant where she works. We had a great time with her throughout the meal. She was very friendly. At closing time, since she was in charge of closing the restaurant, she invited us to stay for one last coffee and talk. We talked about all sorts of things, she told us that she was lonely, didn't have a lover and loved to travel.

We saw her often and our discussions ended late into the night. The three of us have a great relationship and, like us, she loves sex and isn't shy about talking about it openly. This connects well with Fay.

So we meet at her house, on our way back from a trip to Spain, to meet family members she hasn't seen in a long time. Fay is half Spanish on her mother's side and half Quebecois on her father's side. She is 32 years old, quite tall, and has a good sense of humor.

She is 32 years old, quite tall, about 5'7", with long black hair that falls to the middle of her back, beautiful dark eyes, full lips and eternally tanned skin. Her breasts are quite large, but not huge and are firm. Her buttocks are round and plump. She is really beautiful and very comfortable with her body. She is fun and playful, like Flavie. The three of us get along very well.

After an excellent meal, we go to the living room with our glasses of wine. We make ourselves comfortable. I am sitting on the couch and Flavie is sitting on the floor with her back against the couch between my legs. Fay is also sitting on the floor across from Flavie and we chat about things. She tells us more about her trip, which makes Flavie and I dream.

- Did you get laid there? Flavie asks her.

- No...I didn't find anyone hard enough, no one who could fuck me all night without passing out!

We burst out laughing and Fay bursts out with her charming laugh. After a moment she adds:

- Do you know that I have thought about you a lot?

- Have you?

- Yes Tom... I have a confession to make...

I sense an excitement in his face and in his voice.

- What do you have to tell us," Flavie asks.

She hesitates.

- I caught you two fucking....

Flavie and I look at each other in curiosity, a little embarrassed by this confession.

- What do you mean you caught us fucking?" asks Flavie.

- Yes, in that restaurant in Montreal, during a business dinner. I saw you from the back of the room, you didn't notice me. I went to the bathroom, I was in a booth and suddenly I heard a noise. I recognized your voices. I didn't want to make noise because I didn't want to embarrass you and also because I was very excited to hear you.

Flavie and I exchange a slightly embarrassed look.

- Go ahead," says Flavie a little worried.

- Well, I could hear you, I could hear your sighs, your moans... I was very excited. I started stroking myself. My lips were all wet.... I stroked my clit until I came, biting my lips to keep from screaming. I came really hard. Several times later, when I was alone, I stroked myself thinking about this adventure....

My throat goes dry, not because I'm embarrassed by the situation, but because I'm starting to get turned on by watching this beauty masturbate, by watching her cum. My sex slowly hardens. Flavie continues:

- Wow... I'm... stunned... I wasn't expecting this... I'm a little embarrassed....

- You know Flavie, I fantasized, imagining you being taken... that I was there with you.... It really turned me on. Have you ever done it on the count of three?

Flavie's face turns red. She stammers.

- Um... no... well... no, never....

It was the first time I'd seen Flavie bothered by a sexual question.

- Would you like to try it? Here we are, the three of us...I have to tell you Flavie...I want you and Tom terribly.... I really do. You both turn me on.

Flavie doesn't say a word. My sex is now firmly in my pants.

- I don't know, Fay...

- Shhh Flavie... shhh....

Fay moves closer to Flavie and very slowly places her lips on my partner's. Fay pulls her head back a little and looks into Flavie's eyes. Flavie looks at her intently and walks over to Fay and kisses her, this time with her tongue. They kiss passionately, ignoring my presence.

Flavie puts her hands on Fay's large breasts and she begins to moan softly. They continue kissing, their tongues seeking and finding each other.

- Your breasts are firm Fay...I'm horny...really.

- Wait," Fay says.

She stands up and removes her shirt, revealing her large breasts in her lace bra. Flavie looks longingly at those magnificent mounds of flesh and it is she who loosens the clasp between the two breasts to release them. They are magnificent. Quite large, well tanned and look very firm as I watch Flavie gently caress and massage them. They kiss each other more and more.

Slowly, I get up and step back a bit to watch them caress each other. I am very excited. Slowly, I take off my underpants and underwear, then my shirt. I am naked. I walk behind Fay. I say to Flavie:

- I'm excited to see you... a lot.

- Join us," Fay tells me.

I attach myself to Fay from behind and take her breasts in my hands. I caress and massage them. I present them to Flavie for her to lick. She reaches over, sticks her tongue out and slips it over the beautiful erect nipples offered to her.

- Yes Flavie, lick it well...run your tongue around the nipple...very gently, says Fay.... Mmmmm, that's good. I like your soft tongue. Put lots of saliva on it, it turns me on.

I leave Fay's breasts and stand next to these beautiful tits. I stand up and slowly masturbate as I look at them. Fay looks at me:

- 'You are nice and horny. Do you want us to take care of you?

They both get down on their knees. Flavie takes my cock in her hand and as she looks into my eyes she strokes me. Fay takes off her clothes and she too finishes undressing completely. The three of us are naked. Flavie takes my cock in her hand and gently masturbates me. She pulls Fay to herself and pushes her tongue into her mouth. She licks her lips in a passionate kiss, still stroking my taut penis. Release Fay a little:

- Would you like to lick his cock, beautiful? Would you like to suck him...I'd love to watch. I want to see his beautiful cock enter your mouth, I want to see your tongue lick his glans.... It turns me on... Go ahead, lick it, you little piggy....

It's Flavie holding my cock in her hand. Fay takes my glans between her lips while Flavie masturbates me. Fay takes my cock from her hands and sucks me like a fiend, moaning.

- Oh yes...suck it good...suck his beautiful hard cock.... Oh my god he turns me on. I never thought it would turn me on so much.... Yeah, go ahead... Do you like it, Tom?... Is she dirty to your taste? Do you like to see her eating your cock?

- Yes... I like it... suck it well... suck my cock well... you're dirty you know....

Flavie comes over and licks my balls. The feeling is indescribable. Then she walks over to my cock to lick it with Fay. Their tongues lick the entire length of my shaft. I groan to see these two pigs polishing my cock at the same time. I stop them from coming too fast.

- Flavie, do you want to lick my pussy? I dream about it...come lick my lips...eat my little pussy.... I want to feel your tongue on me ...

- I don't know how... I...

- Shhhh... I'll show you.

Fay lies down on the floor and invites Flavie for a 69. Fay immediately puts her tongue on Flavie's lips. She spreads her buttocks wide. I reach down and lick her anus. Flavie moans. I move to Flavie who licks Fay's pussy. She holds her thighs wide open so that I can lick her too. Flavie licks her clit while I work on her labia, vagina and anus. I can hear Fay moaning loudly. Flavie lets out loud moans as well.

- Tom, I want to see your cock enter her pretty little pussy...it's turning me on...come on...I want to see your pretty cock fill her pussy.

I kneel down between Fay's thighs. Flavie takes my cock in her mouth to moisten it and as she masturbates, she caresses our friend's lips with my glans.

- Yes, go ahead, penetrate her.... put your cock inside her... yes... Oh you're eating my mussel Fay...it's good.... do you like the taste of my juice in your mouth?

- Yes, Flavie... I like it when you drip in my mouth... I love it.

At the same time, I push my cock between Fay's thighs and take it unceremoniously. Flavie is busy stroking her clit.

- Aaaaaahhh...the pigs...the pigs...I knew you were dirty too. Yes Tom...stick it all the way in...yes....

After a while I have to pull out to keep from cumming. I'm really excited. Flavie takes the opportunity to grab my cock and sucks me good. She licks Fay's juice off my cock.

- I want you to take me Tom.... Take me while she eats my pussy.... I'm about to cum... Now... Take me!

I move to Flavie's buttocks and with one big thrust push my sex into her hot vagina. Fay continues to lick her clit.

- Yes Flavie...slip your fingers into my love nest. Mmmmm...how I love to see that cock plunging into your cunt.... Aaaahh yes...keep going Flavie...I'm cumming.... Aaaaaahhhhhh.... I'm sinking... lick it all piggy, lick it all.... You want more... Aaaaaahhhh... Yesi.... Aaaahhh...aaahhh...aaaaahhhh.... I'm coming...I'm coming.... Put your mouth on my lips and swallow it all.... Aaaaahhhh...my god it's good.... Are you about to come too? Yes? Come for me...come in my mouth...I can see that big cock smashing your pussy...you're about to come...my tongue on your clit.... you like that, don't you? Come....viens for me... I want your juice in my mouth... Go ahead Tom... faster... he's about to cum the little piggy... Aaaahhh... yes...

I feel a warm liquid running down my cock and into Fay's mouth and she swallows it all. I pull my cock out of Flavie's vagina and push it into Fay's mouth and she starts sucking it unceremoniously while Flavie eats the shell again. Fay comes one more time. Flavie pulls off of her and comes with Fay licking my exploding cock.

- Get on top of her Tom, here...put your cock between her big tits. I want to masturbate you between her big tits.... She turns me on.

Flavie is wild. I sit on Fay's stomach. Flavie stands in front of me, her thighs spread over Fay's face, and Fay starts eating her pussy again. She massages Fay's breasts as she kisses me. She moans... She takes my cock and places it between Fay's voluminous globes of flesh and with both hands glues them together.

- Come on Tom... Work your way between her beautiful tits.... You love her big tits.... You'll cum on her big tits for me.... I want to see you cum, emptying your balls on her chest.

I make my way between her breasts that are all sweaty. This is a good thing. Flavie pulls back from Fay's face and bends down to lick my cock as my glans appears between her breasts, close to the Spanish beauty's face. She kisses it greedily. I'm about to cum.... Flavie is still holding Fay's breasts.

- I'm coming...I'm coming.... Aaaahhh...

- Open your mouth Fay...open it wide...Flavie tells her.

Flavie slides her open mouth next to Fay's so that they both swallow my cum.

- Aaaaaaahhh open...open...I'm enjoying...I'm enjoying...yes....

A big jet hits Flavie's mouth and drips into Fay's. A second shot into Fay's mouth and then a third shot onto the large breasts that Flavie is still holding and fondling. With her hands she spreads the cum all over her friend's breasts as they kiss, exchanging the cum that went into their mouths. I pull my cock closer so he can lick up the remaining drops and join Flavie in licking the cum off Fay's chest. We kiss and Fay joins us with her tongue still full of cum. Flavie and I eat her dirty tongue. It was a very exciting fuck.

We promised to meet again....

A Surprising Gift

I had been living alone for several months, moved to another region, and had relationships with women. I was blossoming and feeling good about myself. My profession allowed me to meet many people and discover many women who, even if they didn't admit it to themselves, wanted gay experiences. I was living with my daughter in a bungalow on the outskirts of a large city and had a very preppy neighborhood. I had made friends with a couple who lived not far from me. They were older than me and we met fairly often. He was an older man, very handsome and very athletic. The handsome 45-year-old man. She was the fashion plate, tall, dark, with long hair, blue-green eyes, a magnificent chest and endless legs. She was 35, a working woman, director of an agency and always dressed very chic and sexy.

Every time we met, I fell in love with her and fantasized about her. How many evenings I would end up masturbating, or when the opportunity arose, I would make love to someone else, thinking very intensely about her. They were aware of my homosexuality, seeing only women in my house, and didn't mind. Real friends, without judgment or prejudice. I wanted this woman more than anything, even though she told me several times that she had nothing against lesbians, she liked men too much to take the plunge. This always made me smile, but this is a personal point of view.

On my birthday, I invited them and some friends over to celebrate my 30th birthday. When they arrived that night, my arms fell off because I found her so attractive. She was wearing a black double-breasted dress with a buckle that opened with every step she took. Her legs were sheathed in very thin black stockings held up by a thin garter belt. A plunging neckline, you could see her generous free breasts, which didn't need a bra. Her dress was tight enough to show off her cute little ass and to show off her curves well. I would have jumped on her immediately if we were alone.

She had a radiant smile on her face and her eyes shone brightly. I walked over and gave her a kiss on the cheek and couldn't help but whisper in her ear.

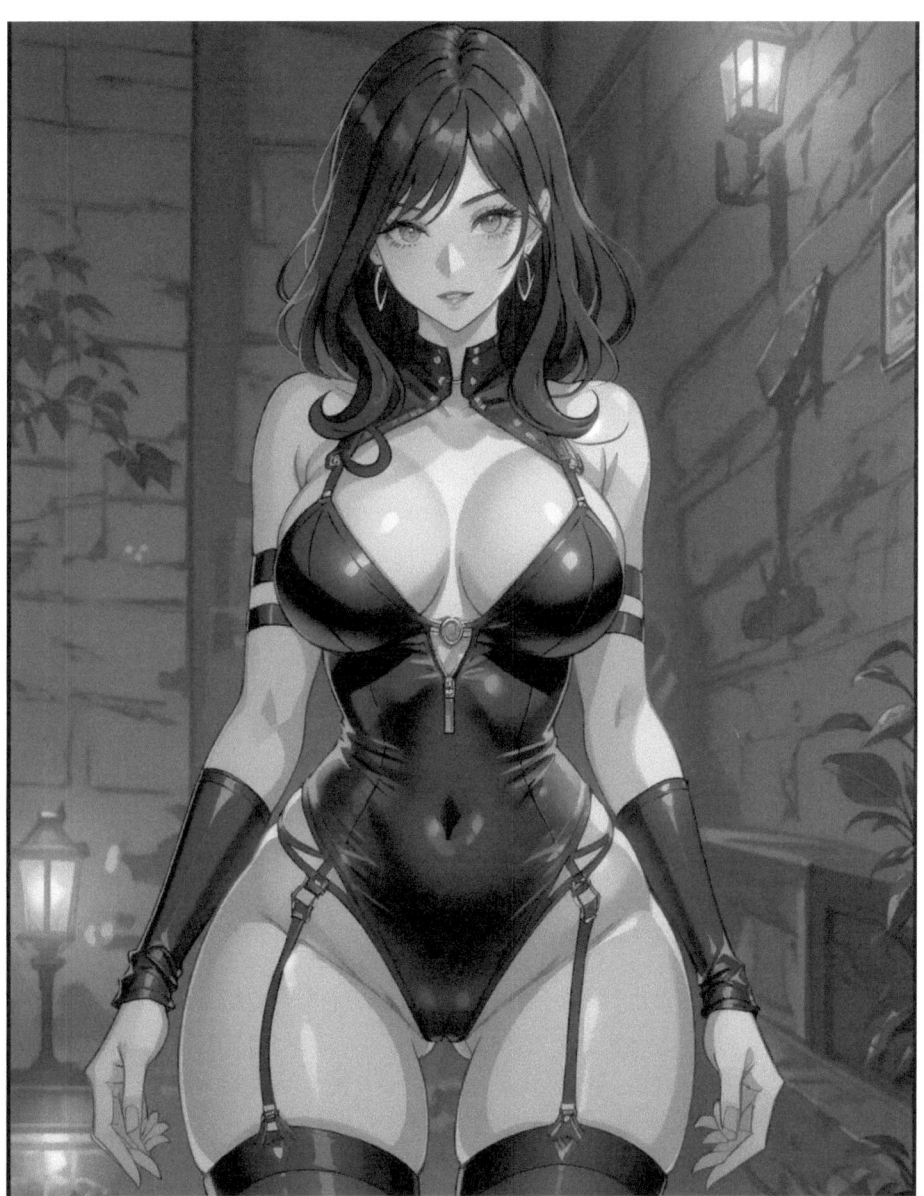

- I see you've already made a down payment, I hope it was worth it.

- A taste of too little. she replied, returning my kiss.

This time the urge had become too strong, I had to pleasure her at all costs, hold her in my arms and make her come.

The evening was going well, the champagne was flowing and the caterer had provided me with a plentiful and delicious cold buffet. The guests seemed to be enjoying themselves and it was time to open the many and varied gifts my friends had given me. In the lot was a very special one, which I must say really touched me. It was a double-belt dildo, nice size, well designed and what's more vibrating for the part intended for the wearer. On the packaging was a small card where I could read these few words.

"Happy Birthday from Emilie and Denis.

This is just a part and we are counting on you to come and get the rest. Big kisses."

I looked up and my eyes met Emily's and she had a big smile on her face. She had a big smile on her face and winked knowingly at me. My heart jumped in my chest and I forced myself not to jump on her. I went over to thank them and her kiss came to the corner of my lips. Denis was truly a gentleman, because even though he noticed, he didn't bat an eye.

The rest of the evening ended quite late and around 1am the guests began to leave. So the three of us were left alone and the house became quiet. Denis had settled into an armchair and was enjoying a digestive. Emilie was standing in front of the couch and seemed to be waiting for something. I could feel her embarrassment and her smile was a little frozen. I dimmed the lights and approached her slowly. I took her hand and spun it around like a waltz. I admired her and couldn't help but say.

- You are absolutely beautiful and you blow my mind.

I placed my hand on her hip and pulled her to me. Our chests joined and I held her tighter to me. My heart was pounding hard in my chest. One of my hands went up her back, while the other went down her rump. Our lips met and our tongues curled in a passionate kiss.

I pulled away slightly and placed my hands on her beautiful breasts, searching for her nipples to roll under my fingers. I had no trouble finding them, they were already erect with desire. Her eyes were closed, her breathing quickened and she placed her hands on mine. I placed my lips on her neck and brushed her from shoulder to ear.

I tried to use the gentlest of gestures, despite my desire to rape her on the spot.

Denis stood up and positioned himself behind her, his hands resting on her hips and drawing her to him. She relented, and his hand came to rest on the bulge that was twisting in his pants. She gently massaged it and he tenderly kissed her on the neck.

My hands traveled down her body, her thighs, her buttocks. I paused to attach the buckle that held her dress closed. Her dress opened and Denis slid it open and dropped it to the floor. I could finally admire her goddess-like body that I had fantasized about so often.

I put my lips on her nipples and sucked on them, and my tongue swirled around them. She let out a moan and her hand came up to crush my head against her breasts. Denis had unzipped his pants and she was running her hand up and down his cock.

I moved slowly down her belly, kissing her and pushing my tongue into her belly button. I continued on my way and found myself squatting down, my head level with her pubic bone.

My hands went to her thighs and I began to gently caress them, kissing them tenderly. She spread her legs to let my head pass and I could put my lips on the inside of her thighs, where the skin was most tender and soft. Denis had grabbed her breasts, which he was fondling, and their mouths were welded together. I placed one of her legs on the couch and gained access to her pussy. My mouth made contact with her vulva, through her thong. Her hand was still accompanying my head as she pressed me against her belly. Her breathing had become erratic and her pelvis was moving slowly.

I undressed, with my mouth still on her pussy, and found myself naked in record time. Denis had her lie down on the couch and propped her head up with a pillow. She was beautiful, offered, willing and ready to offer me her body. I threw myself on her mouth, both hands on her breasts. I covered her with kisses, from her neck to her thighs. I slid the thong down her legs and finally enjoyed the object of my desires. My mouth took possession of her juicy, fragrant pussy and my fingers worked their way into every wet hole they encountered. Her pelvis swayed under my caresses and I could hear her uninterrupted purring.

Denis had knelt beside her, caressing and sucking on her nipples. Two of my fingers had found her rosette and I was beginning to force it in. Her legs were getting wider and wider and she was arching her back to make penetration easier. I pushed one and then two fingers into her anus and began sucking on her clit, exciting it with my tongue. Her hands on my head pushed me against her pussy, her body tensed like an arch and her scream filled the room. I reveled in her dripping onion and worked hard to clean her beautiful pussy. She let herself fall backwards, breathless, stroking my head very gently. Denis kissed her tenderly, still caressing one breast.

I stood up and retrieved the gift she had given me. I wanted her to have the first one. I adjusted it to my waist and straddled her, seeking her mouth to kiss it. She opened her eyes, smiled at me and said.

- That it was good, I never thought it would be.

- I want to take you now and make you come.

- Yes, she said, take me, this is your gift, enjoy it, feel the pleasure.

I moved between her legs, grabbed the hard member and rubbed it against her pussy to lubricate it. She opened up and began to get wet again profusely. I began to slowly work it in, millimeter by millimeter, until my pubic bone made contact with hers. She was breathing hard and her hands clenched on my hips, pulling me into her.

I started a slow back and forth motion and the dildo part in my pussy was giving me an amazing feeling.

Denis, on the other hand, had placed his sex on her lips and I could see his tongue exciting the tip of her glans. She opened her mouth and he penetrated her very deeply, swallowing most of his member. Her hand came around the meaty shaft and she began to masturbate him with great pleasure.

I penetrated him deeper and deeper, I could feel the pleasure increasing and the movements of her pelvis speeding up. I liked to pull my toy out of her cunt to penetrate her better and each time I received a muffled scream from her cock. Her movements became more and more disordered and I felt the end was near. Denis pulled back from her mouth and allowed him to catch his breath for the last gallop. I clung to his shoulders and amplified my movements. He stiffened, his legs tightened around my waist, his belly convulsed and a loud moan came from his throat. It seemed to go on forever.

She was having her first orgasm with a woman.

I pulled out of her, stunned by the pleasure I had just taken, and tried to catch my breath.

Denis was looking at her, a wide smile on his lips.

He slowly came back down to earth, looked at me, smiled and stammered.

- Oh my god, what a pleasure, it's your birthday and you're giving me a present.

- No, it's you, I've wanted you for so long.

- I know, I wasn't thrilled, but Denis managed to convince me. I don't regret it, on the contrary, it was really wonderful.

We kissed tenderly and my hands ran up and down his body, enjoying his soft skin.

I had just satisfied my fantasy and the night was not over. Denis took great pleasure in making love to his wife and she knew how to divide herself between me and her husband, much to his delight.

* * *

As I said before, the night was hot. Emilie gave it her all and Denis discovered an unsuspected side of his wife. We took maximum pleasure, especially me, who had wanted it so badly.

She was my mistress for 2 years and we shared many evenings and nights. Denis shared our nights from time to time, but since he moved around a lot, we were often alone. Whenever we were together, she took real pleasure in teasing me, whether it was with her clothes or her more seductive behaviors.

She wanted to discover everything and encouraged me to go further and further. She had promised herself never to take the plunge, but I was surprised by her behavior. When I pointed it out to her, she simply replied that it was possible to change, and that this experience made her bite the bullet, but that under no circumstances would she leave her husband, who was perfectly happy with this situation.

So I took advantage of this opportunity and shared some crazy moments with her. Every time she felt immense pleasure, especially if the place was risky. We made love in practically every situation, in every place. We looked for the most unusual places every time and often succeeded. There was one situation we hadn't shared yet and I wanted to share it with her. Making love to another woman and I had the right person for this type of evening.

The opportunity presented itself a few weeks later when she was alone for a week. She called me on Thursday to ask me to drive her to the airport, to take Denis with her and she didn't want to make the trip back alone. When I met her at her home, as usual, I was amazed at her attire. She was wearing a midnight blue suit, a tight, straight skirt that came above the knee, very thin flesh-colored stockings, a small garter belt (which she didn't fail to show me between doors), a microscopic, transparent thong, a very low-cut jacket that revealed some of her breasts when she bent over, and perched on high heels that beautifully shaved her leg.

The outward journey went smoothly, and Denis did not fail to emphasize that her absence would not be felt. Given his attire, there was no doubt. We watched him fly away and I offered him a coffee before departing. We sat on a terrace in the airport and I watched her. She was looking all over, looking for a discreet spot, and I guessed what her intentions were. I was amused, but I preferred to interrupt her search.

- Do you mind if we don't go home right away?

- No," she replied, "do you have plans?

- I have a friend who lives on the way home and I'd love to visit her.

- A conquest?

- If you like it, but if it bothers you, let's go straight home.

- No problem, I'm curious.

We laughed and left the airport arm in arm. I had a little surprise in store for her and hoped she would like it.

By Thursday evening I had contacted Marie, who was now living in a beautiful home in the Somme. After all these years I have stayed in touch with her and we see each other occasionally. She was very interested in my proposal and was ready for us. Marie, at 42, was a beautiful woman and did not go unnoticed. She had been my mentor and had introduced me to the joys and pleasures of sex while I was at boarding school.

Around five o'clock, we arrived at her house, she was waiting for us on the steps, a wide smile on her lips. We hugged and I introduced her to Emilie. Marie's eyes sparkled and you didn't have to be a mind reader to see the effect Emile was having. Her wide smile, the sweetness of her gestures and the tone of her voice spoke volumes about Emilie's destiny.

- Hello, you are so exquisite, Juliette has such good taste.

Emily held out her hand, a wide smile on her lips, her eyes fixed on Mary's. "It's true, she really does have good taste.

- It's true, she really does have good taste," she replied.

Marie invited us in and settled us in the living room. Emilie sat on the large corner sofa that lined the center of the room. I sat in a deep armchair across from her and Marie next to me. Drinks were arranged on a small table between us.

Emilie's legs were crossed and her skirt showed her thighs to the edge of the lace on her stockings. Each time she took a drink, she spread her legs and I had a clear view of the triangle of fabric covering her pussy. When she bent over, her jacket would open and reveal her beautiful breasts. My mouth was dry, my eyes were fixed on that beautiful plant and most of all my groin was getting wet. I restrained myself because I had worked out another scenario for this evening.

Marie, as usual, was dressed very chic and sexy in a cream colored suit, stockings and large breasts under her jacket. She was very attractive and knew how to use her charm and power of seduction. I was at the angel, two beautiful women were making eyes at each other in front of me and my voyeur side was satisfied.

Marie was conversing with Emilie, eyes to eyes, and I saw Marie's hand resting on Emilie's knee. She looked at me and, seeing my knowing smile, realized I was happy with the situation and had no problem with it. She sank further into the couch, aware of what was coming, which apparently delighted her. Marie ran her fingers over Emilie's thigh, moving higher and higher to the edge of her skirt. I looked at them and could no longer hear the dialogue, merely nodding my head each time it was spoken to me. My breasts were hardening and my nipples were poking out from under my blouse. I had the urge to fondle myself, but I restrained myself, merely squeezing my thighs together to contain my desire.

Marie put a hand behind Emily's neck and pulled her toward her to put her lips on his. Their mouths opened and their tongues mingled in a deep kiss. Marie's hand rested on Emily's thigh and moved up her skirt. Emilie's hand went to Marie's thigh and caressed her skirt. With her free hand she unbuttoned her jacket and pulled it aside to reveal her breasts. Her breasts were swollen and her nipples were stretched to the limit. Marie left Emily's mouth and moved down to the melons that were in front of her. Her tongue titillated the nipples and her lips sucked on them. Emilie had put her hand behind Marie's head and was pressing it against her breasts; her breathing quickened and she let out a soft moan, her eyes closed. She untied her legs and let Marie's hand rest on the soft skin above her bottom and move to her triangle.

I watched the scene like a movie in slow motion and put one hand on one breast while the other went up my skirt. I spread my thighs and placed my fingers on my soaked vulva. I unbuttoned my blouse and trapped my hard, sensitive breasts. I aroused my nipple with my fingertips and my other hand slipped into my thong. My pussy was wet and my fingers were working on my clit, ready to explode.

Marie had also slipped her hand into Emily's thong and I could see her fingers caressing it from clit to anus. As she passed, she pushed two fingers into her pussy, causing her to sigh with relief. Long moans came from Emily's throat and her pelvis swayed under the expert caress. She had spread her thighs wide to facilitate the caress and was putting on a very exciting show. Her hand behind Marie's head pressed more and more against her breasts, her fingers tangling in her hair. Her desire was not feigned and the anticipation soon won over her resistance. Her moans turned into cries, her body tensed and her thighs closed over Marie's hand, two fingers in her pussy.

I soon followed her into her orgasm, overwhelmed by an endless orgasm. I had taken real pleasure in watching my Mistress being stroked and cumming without restraint.

Marie removed her hand from Emilie's thong and brought her fingers to her mouth to enjoy the powder that flowed from this beautiful plant. She had a satisfied smile on her face and looked at us in turn, enjoying the scene she had set in motion.

Emilie was slowly catching her breath, tucked up on the couch, her hand still caressing Marie's thigh. It took her a long time to come to her senses, a blissful smile on her lips that spoke of the pleasure she had just experienced. Their mouths joined in a tender kiss and I saw Emily's hand tighten on Mary's thigh. Apparently she was letting her know that she didn't want to leave things the way they were and the message went over very well.

After several minutes we adjusted, bright-eyed, and resumed our conversation. Emilie looked at me, grateful, with a tender smile on her lips.

***

Indeed, the evening had just begun, I intended to make the most of it and Emilie and Marie would not contradict me.

We had some well-deserved refreshments and told each other the latest gossip, sometimes very spicy, since our last meeting.

Emilie left to go to the bathroom and I was left alone with Marie. She looked at me with a smile and said.

- I see you still have the ability to find great companions!

- Why should I change, we have the same taste. It's true it's great and I want to share it with you.

- Thank you, I would love to, but you should reassure her, I have the impression that she feels guilty.

- You're right, I'll be back.

I got up and joined Emily in the bathroom. She was leaning against the sink, looking pensive, obviously struggling with something. I walked over to her and put my hands on her hips. She straightened up and looked at me in the reflection of the mirror. I pulled her to me, pressing my chest against her back. I leaned my lips to her neck, which she offered, and her hand came to stroke my hair.

- I feel sick," she said, "I cheated on you, but I wanted it too much.

- No, honey, you didn't cheat on me, I wanted to, I knew what would happen.

- Aren't you mad at me? Marie bewitched me, I couldn't resist.

- I know, she always has the same effect when she wants someone. I don't know anyone who has been able to resist. It's in her nature.

- But how beautiful it was, what an orgasm!

- I saw, my darling, take advantage of it, give it all you've got, I want to see you enjoy and come.

- But you! What are you going to do!

- I'm going to have fun, aren't you against having us both together?

- Oh no!" he replied enthusiastically, "I think I'm going to have fun!

Our lips met and our tongues mingled in consent. My hand went to one breast and I could feel her hardened, taut nipple.

We returned to the living room, where Marie was waiting for us, and in front of Emilie's radiant smile I realized that the dilemma had been solved. I sat back in my chair and Emilie leaned over me to put her lips on mine. She stood up and walked over to Mary, her hand rested on the nape of her neck and pulled her in for a deep kiss. I had an unobstructed view of her cute little ass and started to get wet. This woman was definitely having an effect on me!

She sat back down and Marie put her hand on her thigh.

- Will you stay with me tonight? I'll take you out to dinner.

We gladly accepted, both of us knowing that the evening would certainly not end after the restaurant.

- I know a very discreet one," said Marie, "where we can be alone. I'll go get ready and be right back.

Marie left the room and I moved to sit next to Emilie. I took her hands in mine and asked her.

- 'You don't mind, do you?

- 'No,' she replied, 'I really want to make love to both of you, I'm yours.'

We kissed tenderly, pressed against each other, and inwardly I thanked this beautiful woman for giving me so much joy and allowing me to indulge my fantasies. Maria had just appeared in the doorway and was looking expectantly at the show for us.

We got in the car and drove to this restaurant that Marie had praised. Apparently it was famous, because the owner greeted us warmly. After a few exchanges of trivia, about the weather and the usual introductions, he directed us to an alcove at the back of the room. I took a seat next to Emilie and Marie across from us. The place was warm, cozy and very discreet. The soft lighting gave it an erotic, sensual feel and allowed some privacy without being seen from the room. We had dinner as we discussed, and an erotic atmosphere was growing as the evening went on. Marie looked at Emilie with a tender smile. I put my hand on her knee and pulled it up under her skirt. She spread her thighs wide letting my fingers graze her tender skin over the bottom and reach the triangle of fabric. When my fingers made contact with her pussy, she gasped slightly, which did not go unnoticed by Marie. She smiled at him and his foot came to caress the inside of her thigh, which spread them a little wider to allow the caress. I slipped my fingers into the thong and met a wet pussy, engorged with pleasure. Marie's unshod foot gently caressed her soft skin and Emily's pelvis stirred to the rhythm of the caresses. My fingers sank into her open pussy and her breathing quickened. In the semi-darkness of the room, no one noticed the scene, which added to the eroticism. Emilie closed her eyes, her pelvis tensed and a restrained moan escaped her lips. She was cumming and her pelvis trembled with spasms. She was very dignified and desirable. Mary took her hand and smiled at her.

- Good! You're a cummer, I like that," she told her.

- Much more! I replied, 'When you give, you give it all.

Marie brought her hand to her mouth to place a kiss on it.

- What does she like? Marie asked.

- A lot of things and we don't have enough time all night to shoot.

- It's the weekend, you have free time.

- We're in no hurry," Emilie added, looking at me with a smile on her face.

- 'That's right, you see, I'm following you.

We had coffee and lingered for a while before getting up to say goodbye.

I saw Marie's hand go up Emily's back and down to her buttocks. She was taking the temperature of the atmosphere and testing the firmness of that cute little ass. Emilie didn't mind, she just let her hand wander and seemed to enjoy it. Marie paid the bill and exchanged a few words with the owner. They greeted each other with a kiss and I could clearly see Marie's lips resting on the corner of the woman's mouth. At my amused look Marie said.

- Very beautiful woman, sweet and sensual, a real pleasure.

- You hid it from me! I answered, you have to tell me.

- No problem, I'll tell you.

We got into the car and drove home. Marie was driving, holding the steering wheel with one hand, while the other walked on the thigh of Emilie, sitting next to her. It was a good thing the trip was fairly short because I think she would have had a proper masturbation.

When we got home, Marie whispered in my ear.

- Take her to the bedroom, I'll go first.

She pulled away and I put my hands on Emily's shoulders, pulling her to me. She released her grip and my chest pressed against her back. I knew the house well and grabbed a scarf from a pedestal table in the hallway. I blindfolded her and put my lips on her neck. I brought her arms over her back, trapping her wrists, and led her toward the bedroom. She liked it and obediently let me lead her.

- What's going to happen to me?" she asked, in an amused tone.

- You'll see, be a good girl.

- With you two I expect everything.

We entered the room where Marie was waiting for us, standing in front of the bed. She had undressed and put on a light robe, held up only by a belt at the waist. She had kept her stockings on and the wide neckline that hid only the tips of her breasts made her even more desirable.

I positioned Emilie in front of her, keeping her hands bound, which made her beautiful breasts stand out. I latched onto her and caressed her neck with my lips, lingering behind her ear. She enjoyed the caress and purred with satisfaction. Marie put one hand on her shoulder, under her jacket, and the other on one breast, exciting the nipple with her fingertips. Emily sat up and a cry escaped her throat. Her arousal must have been at its peak. The hand on her shoulder moved to the nape of her neck and drew her to him. Their lips welded together and their bodies pressed against each other. Emily had placed her hands on my pubes and I could feel her fingers caressing me through my skirt. I was getting closer and closer to her and she was standing between us. Marie moved to the side and with her hand on the nape of her neck, went down to her breasts that she was offering. She unbuttoned her jacket, exposing her swollen breasts, her nipples taut as pencils. Marie leaned over and in turn took her nipples between her lips, sucked and titillated them with the tip of her tongue. Emilie arched her back and let out louder and louder moans, trying to get out of the way, so much of the caress made her vibrate. I held her firmly and her fingers worked faster on my pussy. I was getting wet as a fountain.

Mary squatted down and her mouth rested on her pubes. Her hands went to her thighs and pulled her skirt up to her waist. She opened her legs, offering herself to that voracious mouth. Marie tenderly kissed her thighs, over her butt and made her shiver. She slipped on her thong and spread her thighs wide, with one foot resting on the edge of the bed, to better offer her treasure to this intrusive mouth. Marie's tongue made its way between her lips, which she was spreading with her thumbs. Emily twitched, shifted her pelvis forward and let out a grunt of satisfaction. Marie licked her, tongue flat on her vagina, titillating her clit with the tip of her tongue and pushing it as deeply as she could into her anus as she reached her lap. The caress was devilish and few women could resist this treatment for long. Being chained, she had no chance of escape and this quickly increased the increase in her pleasure. She tensed like a bow, a stream of powder flooded Mary's face. Her scream filled the room and her body convulsed. Her orgasm lasted, it seemed, an eternity. Her legs buckled under her and I had to hold her back so she wouldn't fall. Marie kept kissing her thighs and had put her hands on her little ass which she was fondling, spreading her two globes and running a finger over her lap. This only prolonged the pleasure and Emily began to undulate her pelvis again.

Marie stood up and came for Emilie's mouth. I released her hands and her arms went around Marie's shoulders. I made my way to her skirt and slid it down her legs. As he kissed her, Marie slid her jacket off her shoulders, which fell to the floor. She found herself naked, wearing only her garter belt, stockings and shoes. Mary spun her around and laid her on the bed, dropped her robe and lay on top of her. Their lips locked together again and Marie's hands embraced the offered breasts.

I stripped very quickly, keeping only my stockings on, and knelt at the edge of the bed, between Emily's legs. Marie had moved to the side and began to caress her entire body. Emily responded to her caresses, seeking out the sensitive areas, to give Marie pleasure.

My hands and mouth rested on the inside of her thighs, grazing the tender skin with the tip of my tongue. She placed her hand on the top of my head and directed it to her pussy. She was as wet as ever and my tongue went deep into her vagina, one finger resting on her labia. I titillated her anus trying to get my fingers in and she spread her legs as wide as possible to facilitate my entry. I ran my tongue over her clit, sucking it between my lips. The caress made her cry out, muffled by Marie's mouth, and my fingers managed to force their way into her intimate cave. The penetration was all the easier as it was lubricated by the juices flowing from her pussy. Her belly contracted with each penetration of my fingers and her anus grew wider and wider. I wanted to fuck her, but I was giving her another much more pleasurable treatment. Under the combined caresses of my tongue, fingers and Marie's mouth, her orgasm exploded, knocking her down, making her gasp. She collapsed on the bed, devastated, full of pleasure.

Marie and I sat and admired this beautiful woman lying there, submissive and desirable. Our complicity would serve us to offer her an unforgettable night. I wanted this encounter to be forever marked in her memory. We let her recover, because our night was just beginning.

***

Marie stood up, placed a kiss on my lips and headed for the dressing table. She pulled out two nice double belts and handed me one.

- I think you'll like it," she said with a knowing smile.

- You can be sure of that!

Marie looked at me, came over and hugged me tenderly.

- We'll have to spend some time together, I miss you," she whispered.

- 'Yes, I do too.

Our lips met and our hands ran down our bodies in a sensual caress.

- There's some for me!" exclaimed Emily, who had sat on the edge of the bed.

She had held up her blindfold, playfully.

- Of course there's some for you," replied Marie, moving toward the bed.

She leaned over, her hands encircling his face, drawing his mouth in for a kiss. She laid him down, trapping her breasts, which she began to kiss, her tongue running around his nipples. Emily put her hands on Mary's hips and circled her waist. When they made contact with the phallus, she felt its contours like a connoisseur. Her hands felt and squeezed that cock, uttering "Oh! Ah" of satisfaction. She drew him to her so that he could make contact with her soaked pussy, rubbed him all over lingering on her clit, her body arched so that he could reach her roundness. Marie let her, playing along, continuing to caress his chest.

- You love it!!! Do you want me to put it on you, my dear?

- Yes!" she replied, "take me, I want it so much! Fuck me, fuck me!

Marie began to penetrate her slowly, making the pleasure last. Emilie's hands went behind Marie's thighs pulling her into herself, wanting to feel her deep inside. Her thighs were opened as wide as possible and her pelvis was extended to facilitate penetration. Her moans became louder as she continued and began to fill the room.

I lay down next to Emily and took her mouth, pushing my tongue in to meet hers. My hands caressed her swollen breasts, my fingers titillating her taut, hard nipples. Marie had begun slow movements supporting Emily's legs, and she accompanied her with her pelvis. Marie's movements increased, stopping each time she was on the bottom, eliciting a cry of comfort and satisfaction. Emily's body was trembling, her head swaying from side to side, and her hands gripped Marie's bottom. I had taken her nipples between my lips, arousing them with the tip of my tongue, and was caressing her breasts with one hand while my other hand went down between her thighs, rolling her clit, swollen with pleasure, between my fingers. Her pleasure was not fake and her orgasm clicked, shaking her body and filling the room with her screams. Marie continued to penetrate her at the same pace, ignoring her condition, determined to bring her to the peak of pleasure.

I slid my hand up Emily's buttocks, searching for her rosette, wet with pleasure, and pushed my finger inside. It went in easily, I began a back and forth motion in Marie's pattern. I could feel through the thin partition the hard sex, and her cavern opened up considerably allowing me to slide in easily. Marie remained planted deeply in her pussy as I continued to fuck her with my finger. Emily's body shook, her mouth opened, gasping for air. A second orgasm surprised her, knocking her to the floor, and her scream ended in a moan. She fell back on the bed, overcome with pleasure, and lay still for a long time, trying to catch her breath.

Although I was used to seeing her pleasure and cum, this was the first time I had heard her express herself so freely and not hold back her cries of pleasure. Marie slowly withdrew, her pole glistening with wetness, I hurried to clean it and get as much juice as I could from my little darling's pussy. Marie stroked my head, sliding her fingers between Emily's thighs, bringing them to her lips to enjoy the nectar.

We made love to her, all night long, alternating between Marie and me, she experimented with double penetration with two dildos and got immense pleasure from it. She was not stingy with her caresses and knew how to satisfy us, beyond my expectations.

When I woke up in the late morning, Marie was already up, Emilie was still asleep, lying on her stomach with her legs slightly open, giving a very erotic view of her beautiful body and her nice little ass, which had given us so much pleasure.

I placed my hand on her back, tenderly caressing her shoulders. I moved to her buttocks and placed my lips on her loins. The caress must have felt good because her legs spread a little wider and a soft moan escaped her lips, her pelvis lifted slightly several times. I forced myself not to jump on him, my desire for coffee took precedence. I got up, leaving Emilie to her dream, and headed for the kitchen where Marie was preparing breakfast. Her eyes shone with happiness, a wide smile on her lips and the attitude of a woman satisfied after a night of debauchery. We embraced, her lips were soft and tender, our tongues mingled, her hands caressing my back, the small of my loins, ending on my buttocks and drawing me against her. We parted and she offered me a seat at the table.

- It's been a long time since I've had a night like this," she said, taking a seat across from me.

- Oh well! Aren't you satisfied with your conquests?

- Oh yes, I can't complain, but it's been a long time since I've wanted a woman so badly. Thank you for introducing me to her.

- I knew you would like her, I didn't lie to you on the phone.

- You weren't telling the truth, she's lucky to be with you.

- I wasn't sure how she would react, she is very discreet and she really liked you. She wanted you right away, but I'm not surprised, knowing you!

- You don't have to let her go, she is a treasure, beautiful, intelligent, submissive. Isn't your husband too jealous?

- No, I don't think so, he really loves her and sees her happy. And he enjoys it too, she loves it when we do it together.

- It's rare for a man to share his wife with another woman, it doesn't last, he has to enjoy her. One of them is bound to prevail over the other, especially if it is often.

- She doesn't want to leave her husband, she loves him too much, and that's okay. He has already convinced her to do it, at first she was not enthusiastic, but things change and this proves it.

- You're lucky, take advantage of it and give her all the pleasure she wants, it's worth it.

- You are the only person I wanted to share this with and I don't regret it.

- Thank you my darling, I love you, you gave me a wonderful gift, I have to repay you.

- I already have my little idea, we'll see next time.

We burst out laughing, aware of the person in question. We had a nice breakfast and exchanged small talk about our lives and some very juicy anecdotes.

- I apologize, I'll gently wake her up, she likes that. I said after finishing my coffee.

- Go! You know where things are," she replied with a wide smile on her lips.

I went back to the room where Emily hadn't moved and seeing her offered like that sent a sudden wave of desire through me. I picked up the sex toy, which Marie had cleaned, and put it back around my waist. I climbed onto the bed on all fours, my hands caressing her thighs and kissing her from the crease of her knee to her buttocks. Her legs opened, allowing an easier transition to her parting. I spread the two globes and placed my tongue on her rosette, trying to penetrate her. The caress had an effect, her pelvis lifted, giving me a view of her wet pussy and pulsing little hole. A purr of pleasure came out of her throat, as a sign of consent. Her pelvis began a slow back and forth motion as my tongue made its way into her little hole. I licked and squeezed her rosette to moisten it and prepare it for what was to come. I pushed one and then two fingers deep inside her until they slid in easily. She got wetter and wetter, her movements quickened and her purring intensified.

- Oh yes, my darling, fuck me, fuck me, I love it! It feels good to wake up and fuck! I love it.

I stood up, placed my glans at her entrance and pushed slowly, holding her firmly by the hips. Her pelvis met my penetration, until it made contact with my pubic bone. I remained planted low, letting her get used to it, but she didn't see it that way, and began slow movements. His hand slid between her thighs, his fingers titillating her clit, alternating with her pussy. She had raised her head, her mouth open and a continuous sound coming from her throat. I became active, penetrating her along the length of the dildo, which I withdrew to the entrance of her beautiful ass. It slid in and out more and more easily, lubricated by the moisture she was producing. My movements became deeper and faster, I was getting her high and I could feel the pleasure rising inside me. Her fingers penetrated deep into her pussy and came out to finish on her clit. Her movements became more and more messy, it seemed the end was near. Her screams filled the room and unintelligible words came from her throat. Pleasure washed over me, rising from the depths of my belly, and I planted myself deeply into her ass, holding her still, her buttocks pressed against my belly. She immediately lifted up, her body in a frenzy, and his fingers locked deep into her pussy, dripping with juice. Our orgasm lasted forever. I felt her go limp beneath me and I separated from her, only to see her collapse on the bed. It took me several minutes to come to my senses, lying on top of her, savoring that divine moment of pleasure. I moved over, to let her breathe, I placed my lips on her back, caressing her all the way down her back. She was enjoying the caress and had begun to purr again. Emilie got up on her elbows, I was able to reach her mouth, seeking out her tongue and wrapping it around mine.

- It feels so good to be fucked in the morning! she said, I love it. You're going to get me hooked, Denis won't be able to keep up.

- But don't worry, he doesn't give the dog his due!

- What a night you gave me! It was divine, what fun! I didn't think I could have so much fun, you are devils.

Marie had just entered the room and lay down next to Emilie. Their mouths fused together, Marie's hand caressed her belly, all the way to her soaking pussy.

- 'So, little piggy, are we going to have fireworks when we wake up?'

- She said, Oh yes, what a finale, my legs are still cut off. Jealous?

- No, not at all! The next one is for me, if you still feel like it.

- I'd love to, but not now, let me pass, you'll kill me both.

We burst out laughing and took turns kissing, running our hands over each other's bodies.

We spent the whole weekend with Marie, Emilie giving herself completely, experiencing unbridled pleasure, offering her body and caresses for our greatest pleasure. Marie told us about her encounter with the owner of the restaurant and I was able to better understand the qualifications she gave her. I asked Emilie what made her agree to make love to Marie and she replied that she was not indifferent to it, that if she had not fallen in love with me, she would certainly have fallen in love with her, and above all that I desired it very much. I never had the opportunity to share Emilie with another woman again, even though we were together for over a year before she left. I saw Marie many times, she returned my "gift" with Sophie, the owner of the restaurant. I often hear from Emilie, who resumed her straight life and never made the move with another woman. As she says, "It was an intense moment in my life, I regret nothing and it will remain one of my best memories."

AFTERNOON IN GOOD COMPANY

It was three years ago. I was to spend a day with my dearest and most beautiful cousin. I had told her that I had a new girlfriend and she asked me to introduce her on this occasion.

My friend Adeline was eager to meet my cousin Cécile because I had told her a lot about her. To be honest, I lived with her every weekend for over a year and we were very close. My cousin Cecile was a tall brunette with very long hair, and if she wasn't slender by today's standards, her body was superb and harmonious: a beautiful bouncy chest with a small, soft, sexy belly and hips the way I like them. Her long hair framed a Penelope Cruz face. In short, Cecile was truly beautiful and I had a crush on her. And she knew it, which allowed us to play a few dirty games, without really going beyond a few caresses....

Adeline was therefore very happy to discover this very appreciative cousin. We planned to go to an exhibition and a movie during the day and then go back to my cousin's house afterwards to eat.

To introduce Adeline, she was a beautiful blonde with reddish highlights, milky skin dotted with small freckles, big beautiful green eyes, a rather childlike face framed by her long hair. Her chest, if not imposing, was still very beautiful, with a nice curve and very nice nipples that I loved to play with.

Presently, introductions completed and a little coffee grabbed on the fly, we were off for our day of relaxation! The exhibit at the Grand Palais was really interesting and well presented. Then the movie!

We were a little early, so we went to a nearby cafe to chat and pass the time. We talked about a lot of different topics: the studios, the last exhibitions we visited, family, our meeting... and I could feel the girls getting along better and better, despite the small initial tension (Adeline is really very jealous, and the fact that my cousin was so close to her didn't reassure her). Sometimes I would feel a foot brushing against my ankle and attribute it to Adeline, either to call me to order or to mark her territory. This was as far as it went. We talked so much that we lost the session.

It was decided to go back to my cousin's house to finish the afternoon, in the heat and watching a movie if we wanted to. No problem. And then we could have something to eat.

When we got to Cecile's house, she made something quick to eat and while she was doing that, they kept talking. I couldn't get a word in edgewise. Abdicating, I set the table and served a small appetizer to the ladies. The same thing happened during the meal, when I felt like I was just a figurehead. Once the table was cleared, Cécile closed the blinds and turned on the television. We chose a movie to watch and left.

I found myself on the couch surrounded on either side by the two girls. Adeline on my left and Cécile on my right. I savored this quiet moment and put my arms around their shoulders. I heard a small moan from Cecile as I put my hand on her shoulder.

Then the movie began. I was pretty exhausted from my week and was snoozing a bit. I got a few little nudges from my dear cousin who was laughing at seeing me so active. But that didn't make me any more energetic. Soon I felt her fingers playing with my hair, stroking it. It felt nice and pleasant...I let myself do it, with a little moan of satisfaction. I really didn't know where I was or with whom.

His hands went over my face, down my neck, and began to open my shirt. It was true that it was getting a little warm.

My chest was being caressed by these hands and I let go completely. It felt so good... I could feel it slowly flowing through me, but also tickling me at times.... I also felt something strange. But it felt good.

I was sinking further into a very pleasant drowsiness when I felt hands on the top of my thighs... naked! Now I had missed something! And it was the tickling that brought me back to life little by little.... Gradually coming back to myself, I guessed two hands working on my underwear. Not knowing where I was exactly, I thought of that naughty Adeline having a little fun at my expense. And then suddenly I remembered who I was with! Damn!!! I slowly turned to Adeline to stop her from doing anything. We were in the dark, but still!

A hand was still playing with me. I didn't understand now.

Adeline put me back in my seat and continued her games as she whispered in my ear:

- Let go, please. Let's play a little! As she said this, she pulled down my panties and took my now stiff sex in her hand as she licked my left earlobe and told me they were having a great time.

My spirit returned very quickly and I could see the whole scene: a small lamp was on and I could see the room with a faint glow. The girls were in their places, Adeline in her open white blouse and Cecile in her bra, with her sweater on the floor. And their hands were running over my body. My jeans were on my ankles, recently joined by my shorts.

Adeline was jerking me off as she looked at me with a mischievous smile and a little glint in her eye. Cecile wasn't idle, her right hand was caressing my inner thigh and her left hand was moving down my torso.

Adeline stuck her tongue out at me and gently bent down to take my sex into her mouth, but before she did she ran her tongue all over, looking into my cousin's eyes with a look of defiance. Then she swallowed me in one go and started working. I, on the other hand, fondled their breasts and their panties were bothering me and I took them off without further ado. And their beautiful breasts appeared naked to me. I had seen them before, but not together. Adeline's wasn't too accessible, so I took care of Cecile's, fondled her and sucked her greedily. Her nipples soon became erect and she began to sigh. Adeline then looked at me reproachfully, stopped and said:

- No, but oh, it's not over yet! With a serious look on her face. I took her face and kissed her as I let my hands roam over her body. She shuddered and I could see why: other hands were wandering over her body as well. And she had told me about her revulsion for female contact. So I thought that was the end of it. But no! My cousin sensed Adeline's discomfort and left her alone, without first caressing her beautiful breasts.

I continued kissing my better half when Cecile, taking advantage of Adeline's occupation, jerked me off and took me into her mouth, which made me let out a moan of surprise, but also of happiness. Adeline stopped and looked at my cousin as she did so. She was sucking me greedily and with a very nice technique, alternating tongue strokes with a good jerk and mouthfuls. She looked really hungry!

Adeline put her hand on my member and busied herself helping Cecile masturbate me. Then she came down to suck me off too. And there I had my two treasures taking care of me. But, every time I tried to stroke them, they would put my hands or face in their place, telling me that their turn would come later. That I should enjoy the moment. Which I did. I'm usually very resistant during lovemaking and there, my drowsiness increased this tenfold, which made them start to get a little tired. They looked at each other, each took my cock in one hand, holding it straight, and kissed, with my sex between their mouths as they continued their masturbation. This was too much, and I came like never before, cumming widely.

Their faces and chests were smeared with my hot, creamy cum. I couldn't suppress a sigh of intense satisfaction.

And then, to my amazement, Adeline leaned over Cecile to take her property with her tongue, running it all over her face and neck, taking her time. My cousin straightened up and put her hands behind her neck, swelling her ample breasts that glistened with my cum in the lamplight. Adeline stood up and moved to Cecile's right and began lapping at her breasts as she watched me. I couldn't help but suck on her beautiful breasts as well. Cecile moaned and I took the opportunity to unzip her jeans and slip my hand into her panties.

The naughty girl, had partially waxed her pussy from what I could feel. I was pulling out her clit, hard and wet from our little games. I grabbed her jeans with both hands and pulled them down, as well as her panties, to give me the freedom to do whatever I wanted.

My cousin loved cunnis, I knew that and I wanted to do it with her. I stood up, leaving Adeline alone and knelt between Cecile's beautiful, soft thighs.

My fingers roamed and danced over her large wet lips and the pelvic movements I could feel told me I was on the right track. My index finger began to tease her swollen clit and then gently pushed inside her, being careful to make the pleasure last. Given her condition, it wouldn't be long before she came. I then looked into her eyes and slowly moved up to her pussy, gently blowing on it and sticking my tongue out a little. I kissed her and my tongue began its dance, seeking out her intimacy, playing with her small and large lips, tasting her intimate juices. My finger stuck inside her continued her gentle masturbation. Then I irritated her clit so much that she came with a long scream, interrupted by Adeline kissing her fully in the mouth

Then I looked at Adeline, as I continued to lick my beautiful cousin in a very apparent and noisy way. The latter, slumped over, signaled me to stop and turned to Adeline and started licking what was left of my cum on my girlfriend's body. I treated her the same way as

Cecile and removed her pants and thong. We were running out of space on the couch and got up to get comfortable again.

Adeline was naked between Cecile and me. Cecile continued to play with her tongue and I started stroking my girlfriend, which she especially loves when I do it. Her pussy was also soaking wet and it wasn't long before she was blushing and squirming, a harbinger of her orgasm.

My cousin looked at Adeline, but she was no longer there. Then she looked at me, then moved her hand to my better half's crotch, touching it gently and joining me in stroking it. Adeline opened her eyes and watched the spectacle of our two hands working together on and in her soft pussy. And then she came, grunting and screaming like I'd never heard her do, and then closing her thighs in one fell swoop. We withdrew our hands to let her recover. Cecile brought her fingers to her mouth and then tasted the nectar of my beauty with a small smile.

- Hm, that's not bad at all! She then brought my hand to her mouth and sucked on my fingers as she mimicked a blowjob. The slut! She knew I liked it and she could see it by the state of my sex as she stood up.

Cecile put her hand on her sex and masturbated a little, then presented her wet fingers to Adeline's mouth, who swallowed them greedily.

- It's true that it's good! I'll have some more." And putting his money where his mouth was, he ran his hand over my cousin's pussy and licked it greedily.

Finally, the three of us kissed to end our wonderful experience. As the hour approached, we had to leave because Adeline's parents were waiting for us to go to the restaurant....

Our first, and I didn't know it yet the only, experience together was truly a success....

***

I have been with Adeline for over three years now. The beautiful girl, who at the beginning of our relationship was playful and open to naughty games, has given way to a rather uptight young woman who doesn't want to leave the usual routine. Fellatio on the bed or standing, handjobs, cunnis, missionary and doggy style. After that, that's it.

Being very resistant, most of the time I have to finish myself off because she has already cum a lot and can't stand my penetration or rhythm anymore because she's all irritated. In short, she wasn't like that anymore. And very few fantasies: thong only on "party days" (outings, receptions at friends' houses), never with skirts or short dresses, Petit Bateau style underwear.

Despite everything, I remained faithful to him because our relationship didn't stop there. We shared so much and that was worth the noise. Some very pretty girls had already made advances to me, but I had politely declined them, explaining my loyalty to Adeline.

Gradually, it got worse. Not a week went by without two or three fights or reprimands. Then even more often. A few truces softened the tense atmosphere, but it quickly returned. We shared so much, though. Being naturally frank, I told her everything that was on my mind... but most of the time she nodded without really listening or wanting to understand....

Finally, one day I decided to tell her everything, from A to Z, and have a break between us. Of course, she exclaimed that it was all nonsense, that we got along very well, and that she took everything very badly. She left my house in tears as my parents watched her sadly from the downstairs living room.

I was saddened by this myself, but it seemed necessary. Two days later, I got the pleasant surprise of a call from Laure on my cell phone offering me a day out with her in Paris to distract me. Okay, Thursday then! That left me with 4 days....

Laure was a work friend that Adeline had introduced me to and with whom I got along very well. Too well perhaps, as my brother and sister pointed out to me when she came to the house.

I admit that I was very attracted to her because she matched me in character, activities, and interests. She was very different from Adeline, but much closer to me. She was about 5'7" tall, had brown hair cut into a bob, a big smile and a cheerful look. I really fell in love with her facial expressions.

Our relationship was pretty normal until one day I suggested a day out together during a conversation on MSN. Adeline had gone skiing. Laure was on vacation and somewhat inactive and I needed to get out a bit, not having been away with Adeline because I was preparing for a competition. But a day of relaxation never killed anyone. And I really needed it. So, to get back to MSN, I suggested a crazy Parisian day: Big Fish, then an exhibit at the Natural History Museum and a walk in the park. She told me that this was awkward for her in regards to Adeline...I replied that it would be our little secret...I continued with this little ambiguous game...and in the end I was the catch! She ended our discussion with two three more than ambiguous sentences and left me hungry for more until the scheduled Thursday. Wednesday night, I received an email explaining that a work meeting was coming up and she absolutely had to go. And that was it! A story that ended in oblivion and no way to reschedule.... How angry I was.

I threatened her with all kinds of abuse the next time we met, but she calmly explained that she didn't like this kind of game at all. Too bad, I told myself, I like a little of this from time to time....

So no more...

Another plan to make a movie with me, her and Adeline went awry.... Definitely...

And finally this unexpected phone call!

I really didn't want to get involved in anything with her.... at least not at the moment... My orals were fast approaching, my preparation was stagnating, I had a lot of issues to deal with. I didn't need to add to those problems by dating one of my ex's best friends.

On the day, I got ready and arrived at my appointment 5 minutes early as usual. Damn!!! Is it true that he is always late...? Too bad, I put up with the 15 minute delay of the young lady. When I saw her coming out of the subway station, my wait was worth it! Sunglasses in her loose hair, a beautiful smile, a slightly low-cut purple sweater and tight black pants showing off her beautiful legs.

Kisses were a must and we were off! And off we went. A movie in the St Michel district to see a Burton he hadn't seen yet, a Japanese restaurant and then off to the Natural History Museum. After visiting the Mammoth exhibit, we headed to the park to enjoy the beautiful weather. We talked about everything, my recent breakup, my studies, her, me.... It was getting a little chilly and we headed to a nearby coffee shop to warm up and have a drink. A coffee, then a beer for me and a small whiskey, offered by the owner who was a friend. A coffee and a Monk for Laure who said she couldn't stand alcohol at all. The alcohol relaxed me a bit and got me going in all directions of conversation. I told her about the superb classrooms I studied in at the Sorbonne, the Grand Amphi, the Richelieu Amphitheater.... She said she would have loved to visit them, but certainly couldn't. "No problem," she said.

'No problem,' I said, 'you have a student card for this year.

-Yes, of course!

-Well, that's more than enough! Let's go!

I took her by the hand and paid the bill, then we headed for the Sorbonne. The entrance was just a formality and I showed her all the rooms I knew. She was overjoyed!

Eventually we found a small, warm, quiet corner where we ended up with coffee in hand.

We discussed my new single status. She was also single and I laughingly asked her how long it had been for her and what the hardest part was.

She had been single for almost a year. I interrupted her by telling her I wasn't ready to endure a year of abstinence! (It was true, but I think it was the effect of the alcohol that made me say it out loud). She gave a doubtful pout and explained that we did what we could and when all we found were idiots....

-But finally Laure! You're beautiful and pretty and smart and cultured! How so? (an expression I like because it's perfectly French, but often causes reactions...)" with a big smile.

-Well, I don't have much time for that, you see.... my friends have gone right and left... and I don't see many guys interested in me, and when they are, they have a girlfriend," she said with a slightly distressed look.

I stroked her and cupped her face with my right hand.

-And if the girl is gone..." I leaned over and kissed her tenderly.

She pulled back a little, but then let go. Her mouth opened and our tongues intertwined, softly at first, then with increasing intensity.

After a few minutes I pulled away and looked into her eyes. They seemed to be a little clouded by the onset of tears.

- "So what? Is it good?"

-She smiled and stuck her tongue out at me with a wink.

-Ah well, young lady! Well, I'm going to ...and without finishing the sentence, I slipped my hand down her underpants, then directly under her panties to start stroking her pubic area...see this!"

No negative reaction, but rather a small encouraging sigh of the most promising kind. I kissed her neck as I slowly but surely continued to work my way into her panties. Space was limited, so I challenged her with two buttons. My fingers slid over her pubic hair, then reached her labia majora and began stroking them from the outside. I felt tiny contractions along her body. Her pleasure must have been long.... Gradually, my nimble fingers approached her pussy, which I imagine was all wet from my little digital games. Her small lips protruded widely and as soon as my fingers met them, Laure's eyes rolled back accompanied by a small moan.

I dutifully continued my work, attacking the inside of her little pussy, playing with her labia, titillating her clit at times, changing rhythms and techniques. Adeline loved my sessions where I masturbated her for a long time. She said I had fairy fingers and a technique like she had never encountered before. And apparently Laure liked it too.

Feeling her orgasm coming, I lavished her with all my attention an ending she would remember for a long time.

And indeed her hand gripped my thigh hard, digging her nails into my pants, her eyes rolled back and she let out a long moan. Luckily I had the reflex to gag her by kissing her completely on the mouth.

We were on vacation and in a quiet corner, but still students and teachers could walk by and hear us!

I then removed my hand from her pants and brought it to my nostrils to smell her scent which was...um...delicious. Then I sucked on my fingers as I watched her come to life. I winked at her!

-Um... delicious... it's been a while. But I don't remember it being this good! Very different from when I make it for myself" with a big smile and a little wink.

Suddenly we turned around as the revolving door suddenly opened. It was one of my teachers who took one look at me and saw two young men standing next to each other in a tender embrace.

-Well, my dear sir! Although you seem to be in charming company, I would rather have you in the library working on your orals for agrégation!

- "Yes sir, I am thinking about it, rest assured, but this is my fifteen minute break.

- "Very well! It's over," she added, looking at me. Miss, don't blame me, but this handsome young man has his work cut out for him, if I may say so! It's a good thing I'm going to the library. Come with me, you'll help me and it'll only be good for what you have!

- "Okay, ladies. I kissed Laure ardently, looking a little depressed about the tile that had just fallen on me.... I'll be right there."

I left after him, leaving Laure alone in the halls of the Sorbonne.... Pfff, what a lack of luck!

***

After leaving Laure, against my will, in the halls of the Sorbonne, I really didn't know how to continue this new relationship.... The beginnings were promising, but I would have understood if she had taken it out on me for the somewhat? botched conclusion to our first day.

So I called her that night to apologize and to invite her for drinks when she was available.

She told me to pick her up at the end of her class at her school at 5:30 on Tuesday.

-But if I pick you up at the door, Adeline will see me and wonder why I'm there. I'd rather avoid that a little if possible."

- "Take it or leave it."

- "Okay, that's it, you win. But you still don't know what..." with a small laugh and I hung up.

Pffff good, I thought, what could he be up to? I'll see...

I was already thinking about giving her a little gift that I love: a chain for her feet. I find it so sensual... and so one of the first gifts I give my girlfriends.... For the rest of the program, it was more of a very artistic spot...impro certainly...I love it.

The same day I went to one of my favorite stores where I buy all my jewelry and my girlfriends jewelry. I go there often with someone and it always makes the saleslady smile mischievously to see me arrive with a new friend....

I chose a beautiful silver chain, quite simple, but very fine and sensual. The silver looked great with her porcelain complexion. Wrapped up and ready to go!

Five minutes before the exit, I waited by the door and saw a small bulge where I could hide if Adeline came by. I didn't want her to see me at all. What the hell, it was Laure, her best friend, who had told me to wait for her, at the risk of seeing Adeline. She makes do if she needs to, I was going to wait for her at the door!

17:30. It was strange. No noise was coming from the room.... I listened more... Nothing. The little bitch had tricked me! This was a good start!

At that moment a hand patted my shoulder. I turned around and a mouth hugged me wildly and furiously before I even had time to determine the person. Laure! We kissed each other passionately. My hands ran through her soft hair and down her back to tenderly caress her. Hum...what a treat....

She released her embrace and said to me:

- "What a brave knight who was ready to take on grave danger!" laughing out loud "I really didn't know if you would dare!

-I never face my responsibilities. I'm not with her anymore. It was more for your sake that I didn't want to make too many waves. She's your best friend anyway. I don't want to be the bone of contention between you."

- "That's okay." She took my hand and walked up the nearby stairs.

- Let's go," he said with a mischievous little smile.

We climbed the stairs four by four, not really knowing where she was taking me. On the top floor, she headed down the hallway, looking confident. At the end of the hallway, a small ledge would allow us to remain unseen....

She grabbed me by the shoulders, threw me off balance and almost to the back, and before I could react, she unbuttoned my jeans.

-Laure, I love this kind of trip, but here we are at your school, at a time when a lot of people may pass..."

I couldn't finish the sentence because he had already pulled my underpants down and was playing with my underwear.

-See, I can do that even when I have class, she said with a big smile and started shaking the contents of my pants a bit.

Seeing her like this...um she was beautiful and desirable.... I barely had time to look at her. She had dressed beautifully! A little black cover-up with a nice neckline that allowed me to admire a superb landscape, a black skirt and ... tights or stockings! Argg! My second hobby...

She looked at me with the pleading look of a little girl who knows she's about to do something stupid, but that doesn't stop her from doing it.... Her hand penetrated my underwear and her contact with my sex made me shiver. Finally, she pulled down the underwear that was in the way and began to masturbate me gently, then more forcefully.

-So? Sir doesn't seem to be that embarrassed?"

I didn't have time to answer before she moved her lips to my penis and ran them down the length of it, sticking her tongue out once she reached the glans. How good it was.

She dutifully and diligently continued with her fellatio that was truly divine. She modulated her ardor, her tongue strokes and her play with her lips, which she had lustful and very beautiful. To this, she added a whole series of facial expressions and facial expressions that were totally...thrilling!

With my mind elsewhere, I managed to put my hands on her shoulders to alert her to the imminence of my orgasm. She continued to talk. The world could have collapsed around me, I wouldn't have even noticed because I was so excited! Eventually, after trying to delay to get the most out of it, my resistance was crushed and defeated and my orgasm seemed to last forever. Time had slowed down around me. Laure for her part was trying to swallow it all without missing a thing, which she almost managed to do except for a drop coming down from the right corner of her lips.

Overcome by such an orgasm, the likes of which I had never had before, I almost collapsed on the floor. I got dressed fairly quickly. She, on the other hand, was smiling broadly and apparently seemed very happy with her effect!

-So? What do you think, that I lost for 2 years without training?" laughing out loud "I'm not entirely sure. What do you think, just like that, quickly? Does my little warm-up suit your taste? Am I better than Adeline at language games?

Me, a little mocking, and a big liar, laughing:

-Not a bad start, but I hope it will get better! Good potential just waiting to be improved and developed."

He throws himself at me to tickle me by calling me a -big jerk! We continue to laugh and have fun like kids for a few more minutes, kissing.

-I have a little something for you and you seem to have dressed up for the occasion.

I took her by the hand and we walked back into the hallway where a long bench seemed to be waiting for us.

-Please sit here. Here, like this, and don't cross your legs.

She looks at me, a little puzzled. I kneel down in front of her and hand her my little package, which she immediately tears up.

- "Oh thank you so much! What is this anyway?"

I take her hand and kiss it, then grab the chain. My hand starts moving under her skirt, slowly. I feel her shake a little. My fingers continue their descent and now run over her pantyhose (or are they stockings, I don't know yet). My lips have just followed my fingers and are running down her legs. I reach her left ankle, which I massage gently, slowly, taking my time. Then I finally attach her chain. I continue kissing her sheathed legs.

Then I look her straight in the eye. How beautiful she is, full of charm and life. Gorgeous.

My hands move up her legs a bit. I reach up too to kiss her and take her in my arms. Happy. I think we really are. My hands come back down and slide under her skirt.

Wooah! Stockings! Hm... I really like her too much and her mischievous look makes me think she must have known it....

I play under her skirt, touching her crotch, the tops of her thighs, caressing her panties that are increasingly wet. Playfully, I take it off, looking her straight in the eye. She doesn't look very sexy to be honest... but she had lit a fire that seemed to escape her....

I bring it up to my face to smell it... um, what a treat.... Then, I move back a bit. Her face takes on a strange expression, a mixture of curiosity, displeasure, frustration....

-Go ahead, surrender to my gaze. Give me pleasure by giving you pleasure.

-No, that's why you're here. Please finish what you started so well.

The look I give her makes her realize that I am in charge here. She begins to do so, slowly. Her hands untie her wrap, revealing a beautiful black lace bra. She strokes herself slowly, bringing her hands down.

With his fingertips he touches her stockings, gently moving up to her crotch and lifting her skirt. I can then see her beautiful, almost forbidden fruit, well cut with sparse brown hair, but not waxed. Very nice! Then it goes lightly over her pubic area, her large labia. Then I see her wince a little. She slides her index finger between her minimal lips and begins to moan.

Her eyes close in appreciation. I'm in heaven: seeing Laure, half-naked in the middle of a hallway, pleasuring herself, downstairs and with a chain on her feet.... What a pity not to have anything to immortalize this image....

With his right hand he spreads her labia majora so that his left hand plays with her labia minora, her clitoris and the entrance to her vagina. Her pussy is now soaking wet. Deciding that I had left her alone to play enough, I quietly moved in closer. I think she left anyway. Gently on all fours, I came within a few dozen inches of her apricot.

She brought her left hand to her mouth, which she then opened to taste its nectar. Taking advantage of the opportunity, my mouth took the place of her absent hand. She grunted when my flattened tongue moved all the way in, swirling in places.

When I reached her clit, I teased it with the tip of my tongue, playing with it, sucking on it a little, sucking on it. My hands did not remain idle and caressed her legs, her belly, her still trapped breasts.

As I like to do, I took my time, to make it long, to make her come slowly, but surely, little by little, to make her beg to finish. Sometimes I would get close and kiss her, making her share her precious, good nectar.

Finally, I decided to finish her off in style. I penetrated her intimacy with my right index finger, while I had freed her breasts from their shackles and began to caress her with my left hand. My tongue continued to be playful, but became more precise, more skilled, more regular and more supportive as my index finger picked up a rhythm close to that of my tongue.

A few seconds were enough to see her sit up, her eyes rolling back, moaning louder and louder and screaming loudly, letting herself fall backwards.

Having perhaps her scream alerted someone, I quickly sat down next to her and kissed her fiercely, not letting her recover too much from her emotions, and wrapping my arms around her so as not to expose her chest too much in case...

Finally healed, she told me:

- "Potential, no doubt, but still needs some practice to fully express herself. Honorable mention," laughing.

How beautiful she was when she laughed. Even more beautiful than when she came. I was under her spell. She got dressed, grabbed her things, and we headed for the stairs.

When we reached the glass door separating the hallway from the landing, we met Marie, a friend of Adeline and Laure's, very pretty with very fine facial features, who watched us walk arm in arm, smiling, as happy as we were. We chatted for a while and then went our separate ways.

It was then that I thought I caught a glimpse of Marie's wink at Laure....

A BEAUTIFUL DAY

This story is a true story that happened to me in May 2011. I live in a village in Alsace and it was a beautiful sunny day.

I was at home, my husband was at work, I was taking care of the house, cleaning, tidying up, gardening, when around 4pm the doorbell rang. I opened the door and a woman came in.

Marie: "Hello ma'am, my name is Marie Wagner, I'm a salesman, I could take 15 minutes of your time and show you what I do and sell."

I let her in, I had nothing in particular to do, and since she was a woman, I was less suspicious, a man wouldn't come in. I sat her down in the living room and offered her a drink. I looked at her, she was a beautiful woman with a dull complexion, short black hair, I would say 40-45 years old, dressed in a nice suit, the kind of suit all commercial women wear, and a pair of stilettos.

Marie: "I won't take up too much of your time, I work for a company that sells lingerie and erotic gadgets to your door. In fact, I'm looking for people who would like to throw house parties by inviting friends and acquaintances. I come to present and sell.

Me: "Why not, it could be original, I should see if any friends would be willing to come."

Marie: "Of course you can have a lingerie night, or a sex toy night as they say, or both. The organizer will get a gift, a lingerie set, an erotic gadget or both if we make it a party for both.

Me: " I don't know, like I said I'll see, I confess it will be the first time for me, I'm not very used to it".

Marie: " But if you have time to spare, I can show you some of the pieces and catalogs, so that you can see and sell better, at the meeting, to your friends ".

Since I had time on my hands and my husband would not be home until about 7:00 pm, I agreed, since it would keep me busy at the end of the afternoon. Marie went to get two suitcases from her car and returned, opened the first one and pulled out several pieces of lingerie, sets, thongs, shorties etc. ....

Marie: "Here are some pieces from the collection, for the evening I will have more. If you like any of them, let me know.

I wore a black lace set, thong and bra. She offered me to try it on. I said to myself why not. I went into the bedroom to try it on. Then she asked me if I liked it and to come over and tell me what she thought. I didn't dare, being rather shy, but she was a woman and must have been used to it. I stood across from her in the living room.

Marie: "That dress looks great on you, I'm sure your husband would fall in love with it right away. Let me adjust your bra, the straps aren't quite right.

Before I could respond, she stood behind me and began adjusting the straps. She was on my back, I could feel her breath on my neck. Suddenly she said to me:

Marie: "you know you are a very beautiful woman, your husband is lucky and I promise you moments of pleasure in this dress".

I was embarrassed and petrified by this situation. I was not used to this kind of talk from a woman.

Marie: "I think you are very desirable and this dress fits you perfectly, gives you a lot of class and shows off your chest and buttocks.

As she said this, she pressed herself against me and took one of my breasts in each hand. She began to tenderly caress them. She placed her lips on my neck and gave us light kisses. I seemed to be stuck, not reacting.

Having an experience with a woman had crossed my mind before but I had never imagined doing it. Her hands roamed over my chest, the caresses becoming more and more intense. I didn't know how to react, it felt good and very awkward at the same time.SHe removed my breasts from the hold of my bra and began to play with my nipples which, under the insistence of his fingers, began to harden and swell. Se kneaded them, rolled them under his fingers, pinched them. Then, as Se played with my breasts, he lowered the other one to my lower abdomen. Se passed it under my thong and reached my sex. He began stroking my buttercup, jerking it. To my surprise, my lower abdomen began to feel warm and wet. Then she said:

Marie: "I can see that what I'm doing to you doesn't leave you numb. Let me show you another piece of my collection.

Marie let go of me and took off her shirt and dress. She was standing in front of me in a beautiful white suit. A bustier attached to black silk stockings, a thong. She was also beautiful in this outfit. It didn't leave me indifferent. Then she came up to me and kissed me on the mouth. I felt her tongue insist on my lips to open them. Without knowing why my lips opened and our two tongues met. She took my hand and placed it on her breast. I began to caress her and the more I caressed her the more I felt my sex get wet. After a long, fiery kiss, she took me by the hand and laid me down on the couch.

She took off my thong and started licking me, it was beautiful, different from my man. More tender, more affectionate and above all more sensual. I could feel his tongue circling my clit, playing with my lips. I loved it, I've never felt so aroused. She knew how to do it, it wasn't her first time. Then she started playing with her fingers, she introduced one then two fingers. The more she touched me, the wetter I got.

Marie: "So Caroline, this is not good, I like you, you turn me on, I want you too much.

After a few minutes of this torture, she got up and opened the second suitcase. Inside were a lot of gadgets, dildos, ducks, geisha balls etc. .... She took a dildo and said:

Marie: "You'll see, it's not worth shit, but this toy is my favorite in the collection, I've tested them all."

She took the dildo and penetrated me with it, inserted it, removed it, inserted it again. What a treat, then he put it on, and there the vibrations of this toy made me cum in a few moments. Then he took a second one and presented it to my anus. Without asking my opinion, she introduced it, I who always refused sodomy to my husband, I was taken in the moment, in the desire. She left the first dildo in my still vibrating pussy and fucked me with the second in my ass. I had never cum like that. I didn't know where I was, my first experience with a woman was unforgettable. But with all these moments of pleasure I didn't see the clock ticking.

Suddenly the living room door opened and I saw my husband standing there. He saw me half naked, a dildo in my pussy and a stranger dilating my ass at the same time. I didn't know what to say, I was like a child being caught doing something stupid. He too was fascinated by what he saw and said:

Kevin: "I see some of you are having fun while I'm working. Good for you. Some people are struggling at work and some people are having fun. Also, you are doing things that you refuse me. And who is this woman?"

***

Without backing down, Marie stood up and walked over to Kevin to introduce herself.

Marie: "Hi, my name is Marie and I'm a salesperson, I was introducing some items to your wife and in the mood I had them tested. I hope you don't mind.

Kevin: "Let's just say I wasn't expecting it when I got home, and especially not from my wife.

Marie: "But now that you're here, wouldn't you like to join in, Caroline is all hot and I haven't gotten anything yet. And a good cock is better than a sex toy.

I couldn't believe how shameless and unashamed this woman was, a real little devil under her airs of being a good woman. Kevin didn't know what to say, he was speechless and remained motionless in front of this woman. Without wasting any time, Marie went over to Kevin, unbuckled my husband's belt, opened the jeans that fell at his feet, pulled down his pants, grabbed Kevin's sex and began to masturbate him with her expert hand. It didn't take more than a few seconds before Kevin's sex was stiff and taut, she unfastened it, got down on her knees and took his sex into her mouth. She sucked him in front of me, without any remorse.

She devoured his entire sex, I could see her mouth going back and forth on my husband's member, her tongue circling the glans and licking the entire length of the cock. Kevin had closed his eyes and was enjoying himself. I have to admit that seeing this woman sucking my husband's cock turned me on more than it made me angry. I grabbed the dildo I still had in my sex and started masturbating with it. She stood up and completely undressed Kevin and took his hand.

Marie: "Come with us on the couch, you will fuck us, your cock is very good, and very hard, just the way I like it.

Marie sat down on the couch and Kevin stood in front of her, she resumed her fellatio. He spit on the glans and sucked with pleasure. Then she told me to join her, it felt so good. She handed me my husband's sex and while she jerked him off I started sucking him. Kevin was ecstatic.

We took turns, once me, once her, two mouths just for him. Our tongues crossed over his glans. Having never had this experience, it didn't take long for him to cum in both of our mouths. Marie's lips were full of cum, as were mine. She smiled at me and leaned in to kiss me. We kissed, full of cum, and it felt good. Then she started licking my breasts, I did the same, she had smaller breasts than mine, but much bigger nipples. In turn I took the initiative and stroked her little pussy which was completely shaved, compared to me who was quite hairy. Faced with this lesbian scene, it didn't take long for Kevin to get hard again. We decided to go to the bedroom.

Marie lay down on the bed, Kevin got on top of her and started to penetrate her, I laid down next to her and licked her breasts, she played with her clit. The three of us had never done this before with Kevin, but it felt like it was natural. After a moment, Kevin pulled out his sex, I leaned back on the pillows, Marie got between my thighs and licked me while presenting her ass to Kevin. This one, without being asked, took her doggy style, I saw her face full of happiness. Having never wanted to be sodomized, he took advantage and sodomized Marie, this one said nothing to the contrary.

This woman exuded an unbridled desire for sex. Kevin took advantage of this and pounded her like never before, alternating between her pussy and her ass. Marie came with loud moans. Then it was my turn, I had never seen Kevin so powerful, I didn't recognize him. He penetrated me and gave me everything he could. Marie lay down next to me, we kissed, fondled each other's breasts, Kevin went from one woman to the other and gave us much pleasure. Feeling her moment coming, she stopped, searched the living room for the two dildos we were both playing with, then inserted a dildo into each of our pussies. Now he was fucking us at the same time, I was soaking wet from it, Marie and I were moaning, the more he dilated us, the more we screamed. I think we both came at the same time. I had never had so many orgasms in one day. Kevin was taking the opportunity to cum between the two of us and slide his sex over both of our breasts, playing with his glans and our nipples. We tried to take his sex with our lips, our tongues sometimes touching his glans, then we got Marie and I on all fours, Marie was fucking me with the dildo, while Kevin was fucking Marie again. He enjoyed this bastard well, and in a few minutes he cum in Marie's bottom when he pulled out his sex, we saw the cum running down Marie's legs.

After all that pleasure, Marie got dressed and told me to keep my lingerie set and the 2 dildos we played with. It was her gift for all this shared pleasure. She left me a card to contact her and she kissed Kevin and I and left as if nothing had happened. To this day I have never contacted her again and I didn't want to. But I was torn between wanting to see her again and the embarrassment of that day.

That night, Kevin and I had been fucking all night. This had turned us on terribly and opened a new door in our sexuality, which until then had been quite normal, even mundane. That night I accepted Kevin's pleasure, all his desires, he sodomized me, did a double with the dildo, fucked like a bitch. And he was right, the lingerie set was a huge plus for him. Since then I don't fuck without a good sodomy, my sex life has changed forever.